Muriel

Muriel

CHARLES HAYS

authorHOUSE®

AuthorHouse™
1663 Liberty Drive
Bloomington, IN 47403
www.authorhouse.com
Phone: 1 (800) 839-8640

Published by AuthorHouse 01/18/2016

ISBN: 978-1-5049-5240-8 (sc)
ISBN: 978-1-5049-5239-2 (e)

Print information available on the last page.

Any people depicted in stock imagery provided by Thinkstock are models, and such images are being used for illustrative purposes only. Certain stock imagery © Thinkstock.

This book is printed on acid-free paper.

DEDICATION

This book is dedicated to the greatest English teacher that a young high school writer could ever expect to have. She came to Eastern Kentucky from Columbia University with a desire to make a difference in the quality of education for the Hazard High School students. And, she did, most certainly.

Mrs. Emma B. Ross

On the way to Hazard from Columbia, she and her husband suffered a horrible car wreck. He was killed but, she survived the ordeal and she taught at HHS until her retirement.

FOREWORD

In the coal mining business, there were many Coal Barons but, very few Baronesses. This book which I have just begun and hope to soon finish is about the only Coal Baroness that I have ever known. Her name was Muriel Combs and she was a ninth generation relative to Elijah Combs, the original settler of Hazard, Kentucky. It was a real pleasure to have known Miss Muriel and I will always respect her and remember her for her raw courage in fighting for her own rights against all of her male business competitors. And, if you think that the coal business was an easy task for her, think again. It was not exactly female-friendly during a time when women were expected to remain in the kitchen or the bedroom.

CONTENTS

Chapter One

YOUTH

Muriel Combs and I were star-crossed-lovers from the very beginning of our relationship in the Fall of 1938. The September of that year was when we both signed up for classes in the first grade at the Lower Broadway School of Hazard, KY. Muriel lived in Lothair, KY and I lived in North Hazard proper. This also meant that she was born in 1932, just as I was. Beyond that, neither one of us knew which one was the oldest of the pair. And, we didn't worry very much about that sort of stuff at such an early age.

But, we did like each other very much and we two were often observed as hugging and kissing, like they do on the silver screen of the Virginia Theater that existed on Main Street. We were noticed by many and most of them viewed me as the young kid who was trying to advance beyond his station in life. And, that situation does require some explanation.

Muriel Combs was born with a 'silver spoon' in her mouth. She was a ninth generation relative of Elijah Combs, the original settler of Hazard, KY and Perry County, KY. And, her own father owned considerable holdings in the coal fields of the entire area surrounding the City of Hazard, from Allais and Wabaco to Leatherwood and far beyond, almost to Whitesburg or Corbin, a distance of 73 difficult miles. He was a rich man who could buy and sell mineral rights at the drop of a hat.

It was Muriel's grandfather who financed FDR's presidential campaign by purchasing all of FDR's mineral rights just prior to his campaign run for the office of President of the United States. Franklin D. Roosevelt needed a large amount of cash money to finance his campaign expenses against incumbent Herbert Hoover in March of 1933.

That last statement also explains our 'star-crossed' descriptor; because our relationship was destined to be often hampered by external forces. She was one of the richest young girls in town and I was one of the poorest boys that was available because I represented 'poor white trash' from a railroad laborer's family. In brief, I was everything that she wasn't since we both came from very different sides of the railroad tracks. She represented the high end of society while I symbolized the lowest end of the same group. And, this be the case very often for many couples because 'opposites' always seem to attract each other, don't they?

We were both born during February of 1932 while the Great Depression of 1929 was still running rampant in The United States of America. And, that depression didn't really end until the time that WW-II was initiated, in September of 1939 when Hitler's soldiers marched into Poland.

Yes, Muriel and I first met at the Lower Broadway Elementary School in 1938 when we were each required to give up some of our civil liberties because some high-classed individual had passed a low-classed law saying that all children were required to attend school classes for twelve long years. At first, that sounded like an evil prison sentence. But, I will admit that, with more time, school became much more interesting for both of us and all of the other students in my hometown. Our wonderful teachers made it so.

Of course, I was forced to give up my fishing and hunting habits while sweet Muriel forfeited her own creative talent of sewing beautiful rugs together as a hobby. That extra income had created some extra spending money for her personal needs and higher priorities, like those delicious chocolate milk shakes from the Rexall Drug Store fountain.

Yes, we both met each other in the first grade of school. She was living in Lothair, KY at that time and she rode her horse to school each and every day. That beautiful stallion was very high spirited just as Muriel was. So, she and her horse (High Cloud) made a peaceful pair and a very likeable image.

Originally, Cloud was a young thoroughbred from Calumet Farms of Lexington and Muriel was, at all times, in full control of her horse. The worst scare that either of them ever had was when a rattle snake tried to attack High Cloud but the snake was just too slow for that lively stallion. Just one strategic stomp and that snake became as dead as a door nail.

I was overwhelmed by her youthful beauty and her natural charms. To my way of thinking, she was the prettiest student of the entire lot. I volunteered as her protector and her helpful bodyguard. And, there were several occasions where I had to fight some of the other boys to prove that she was mine and mine alone.

There was a large shade tree on the Lower Broadway School playground and that's where she taught me how to kiss. Some people say that kissing is a natural thing and that everyone does it slightly differently. But, I can tell you this much about Muriel's kissing ability. It was way beyond ecstasy and that made a six year old boy quiver to his innermost soul. I was too young to know very much about foreplay. But, I was willing to learn and Muriel was determined to properly teach me the beginning tricks. God bless that lovely young girl as I am very grateful for her early teachings. Here, I am reminded of some old lyrics which do apply and they are listed as follows:

> *Look what you did to me,*
> *Thank you for doing it.*
> *Look what you did to me,*
> *Thank you for doing it.*

Sometimes, our very interesting conversations about love, marriage and children would also involve realistic discussions of what was going on in the outside world that surrounded us; namely, the war in Europe and that terrible stress upon our soldiers. My Uncle James Homer Hounshell was one of the first to assault the beaches at and near Normandy. And, of course, we could never forget that still lingering financial depression.

On October 29th of 1929, Black Tuesday had struck Wall Street as stock investors traded about 16-million shares on The New York Stock Exchange in a single day. Billions of dollars were lost, wiping out thousands of investors. In the aftermath of that Black Tuesday, America and the remainder of the industrialized world spiraled downward into the Great Depression (1929-1939), the deepest and the longest-lasting economic downturn of the Western industrialized world up to that particular year in history. In school, we were taught the following about how that awful depression affected the rest of the world; namely, the industrial nations.

BRITAIN: The effect of our Great Depression on the industrialized areas of Great Britain were immediate and devastating since the demand for all British products collapsed immediately or almost overnight. And, the negative rate of change for this phenomenon could not be altered or changed by anyone.

FRANCE: The Great Depression began to affect France around 1931. France's relative high degree of self-sufficiency was considerably less as compared to that for Germany. However, hardship and unemployment did lead to rioting and the rise of the Socialist Popular Front.

GERMANY: The Weimar Republic was hit very hard by this world depression as American loans to help rebuild the Germany economy were now stopped completely. The unemployment soared, especially in the larger cities where the unemployment rate reached 30% during 1932. and the political system veered toward extremism when Hitler's Nazi Party came into power in January of 1933.

JAPAN: Our Great Depression did not strongly affect Japan because Japan's Finance Minister was wise enough to introduce deficit spending and to devaluate the currency at exactly the correct time.

RUSSIA: The Soviet Nation had no stock market so they were somewhat insulated if compared to the financial problems of the other aforementioned countries. And, their narrow-minded ways served to protect them against any pending or extensive disasters.

As WW-II approached, Muriel and I both tried to understand the effect of this war which would lead to the death of 70-million people before it ended in 1945. As two very young analysts, our main concern involved this question, what did President Franklin Delano Roosevelt do that helped to turn the tide of victory over this nasty economic decline?

- FDR raised the Minimum Wage,

- FDR improved the Public Works,

- FDR introduced Farm Subsidies,

- FDR destroyed existing crops and livestock to prevent surpluses.

- FDR invented the Securities and Exchange Commission to oversee the stock market.

- FDR attacked unemployment by forming the Civilian Conservation Corps.

- FDR began the Tennessee Valley Authority for controlling floods and creating electricity for public power.

- FDR installed Trade Association agreements to help raise prices.

- FDR started the Industrial Recovery Act that led to the Works Progress Administration.

- FDR and his new innovations did not end or abate the suffering of the people. But, they did significantly help millions of Americans.

- FDR entered WW-II to help the British defeat the Germans.

FDR was our greatest President ever and, without any doubts whatsoever. Yet, we rarely honor him enough as we ought to do. We two students do hereby propose that there should be a day set aside to give FDR the praise that he has earned. And, when we turned this student essay in to our teachers, we both got a grade of A+.

In brief, FDR saved this Nation for all of its citizens both then, now and beyond. What more could any one person have done for his native Country? He was a victim of polio yet he managed to fulfill our grandest hopes; to get rid of the Great Depression and to win World War II. Now, we must give FDR's gigantic spirit a personal favor:

- We must do whatever we can to never allow such a thing to ever happen again.

At this modern time, greedy hands are, once again, playing with our currency. May God be with each of us as the upcoming years advance toward each one of our homes and families. And, I sincerely pray that no young author or authoress will ever have to suffer the deprivation and hardships that came in my direction.

Chapter Two

HIGH SCHOOL

In 1946, Muriel and I both moved on to that great event where we each became enrolled in the Hazard High School System for the very first time. We had mixed feelings about that great challenge which loomed before us and in our near term future. Some of those worrisome concerns of ours are listed as follows:

1) Just four more years to go before we each entered our young adulthood.

2) We were both well past our puberty restraints so, we could do whatever we wanted, whenever we wanted to or so, we thought.

3) We each feared the well-qualified Faculty and Staff that were graduates of Columbia University and other similar Institutions.

These talented people were each lured to Hazard High School by cash rewards which originated from the earnings of different Coal Barons and Baronesses. This is to say that HHS had one of everything and two of most. These luxuries were affordable because of all those generous grants from the local business men and women who served as our very active 'sponsors'. And, we were also great in all sports because of the tremendous wealth that was derived from the profits that Black Gold generated. We were financially able to import great athletes from as far away as Northern or Western Kentucky, young men like the fabulous and unequaled quarterback Jerry Hines or the tenacious linebacker Ray Henry, among many others. For example and after the end of WW-II, football coach Earl Collins had the heaviest line that ever played football for Hazard High School and we were, of course, undefeated during that entire season.

4) Because our faculty and staff were so talented, it seems that we ought to include their likeness for eternity. It seems fitting that this author should attempt to preserve their memory for perpetuity, especially since I recently read on the Internet that one female student of the 1940's went to HHS without ever knowing any teacher named Emma B. Ross. How was that even possible? Every citizen in Hazard knew that kind lady. She was the dean of girls and a grandmaster of the English language.

5) It has been written that a successful school operation depends upon three different requirements; students, space and staff. Another measure of success is the rule which requires that the student- to-teacher ratio (STR) be less than twenty to one (20:1). At HHS, our STR was (15:1) which greatly helped Hazard High School to become one of the top ten rated schools in all of Kentucky. And, as the students perform better, everything else follows on a successful pattern in associated manner. Good behavior creates better results and better results produce sheer perfection.

6) Since the Staff made the school so outstanding and, because the Staff also created such brainy students, it is highly appropriate that we honor the Staff at this late date, even though most of them have long since passed away. They might be gone but, I assure you, that they are not forgotten by any of their former students. Rule Number 39 of Life: Never forget what you were taught and long remember your teachers. They worked very hard to make you successful. It is a personal honor and privilege to present the following photographs:

The Faculty & Staff Of Hazard High School In 1946-1950

Roy Eversole, Superintendent of Schools
Background: Business

E. D. Brown, High School Principal
Background: Military

Lester Eversole, Secretary
Background: Hazard High School

Edna Barnes, Home Economics
Background: University of Kentucky

Richard Asher, Attendance Officer
Background: Hazard High School

Earl Collins, Math & Football Coach
Background: Georgetown University

Homer Osborne, Basketball & Baseball Coach
Background: Eastern University

Emma B. Ross, English
Background: Columbia University

Geraldine Mattingly, English
Background: Syracuse University

Nannie Belle Kelly. English
Background: Transylvania University

Elizabeth Griffey, Typing
Background: University of Kentucky

Alvin D. Shelton, Chemistry
Background: Eastern University

Ira J. Francis, Physics
Background: Morehead University

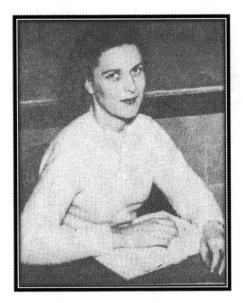

Faye Arnett, Government
Background: Wellesley College

Anna Roberts, Librarian
Background: Eastern University

John D. Bowling, Social Sciences
Background: Eastern University

William Walter Hall, Band Director
Background: Curtis Institute of Music

Dicey Jane Callihan, Biology
Background: Eastern University
(NOTE: There is no existing photograph for Miss Callihan
so, this is a model illustration from Thinkstock.)

On the other hand, we were both very excited and quite anxious about meeting the prestigious high school staff and listening to their lectures. Hazard High School offered eighteen classroom teachers and fourteen of them each possessed diplomas from other colleges in or out of the State of Kentucky. Folks, that represents a total percentage of almost 80% of the teaching staff to be holding a college degree, a fact that was unheard of in those ancient days.

This is to say that we admired and respected our teachers because neighboring schools weren't nearly as fortunate. They had teachers that read books to their students while we had trained scholars and intellectuals. In that regard, we were blessed and, for most of us, that one fact paid off in huge dividends. We students of HHS were much smarter than those of the nearby counties.

The fact that Muriel and I were most interested in was that we would soon be labeled as graduates from the Hazard City School System and then, we would be on our own, free to do whatever we wanted or whatever the law might allow us to do.

However, after about two years of lectures, those high school courses became suddenly, no longer simple and almost everything that was taught was suddenly made unnecessarily complex or, at least, quite boring and, sometimes, positively troublesome.

For example, the lecture periods of chemistry and physics were well described but, not fluently understood by any of the students. We just suffered through those awkward presentations and accepted whatever final grade we received as being appropriately kind and far more than any of us students really deserved.

However, Muriel and I did replace our first shade tree with another one of like kind. And, here, the act of kissing was now just a preliminary event for what was called foreplay.

Both she and I enjoyed this change of pace as she lectured me on the wisdom of using a condom during our intercourse sessions. Did you know that condoms were first invented in 1000-BC when the ancient Egyptians used a linen sheath for protection against syphilis? Muriel was the most intelligent girl that I ever knew so, I was quite willing to relax and let her play the leading role and the controlling influence for our virtual adult relationship.

Chapter Three

FACTS

The bituminous coal mining business is, by itself, not very complicated. It depends on demand and supply just as most other businesses do. However, it is strongly seasonal in the sense that no one needs to heat their home in the summer time. Perhaps, a few more facts about the coal business will shed more light on the business and some of its associated complexities. Consider the following facts:

- Coal is the most abundant fossil fuel throughout the entire world.

- Experts claim that adequate coal reserves will be available for another 220-years.

- Global recoverable reserves have been estimated at more than 1000-billion short tons of coal.

- The United States accounts for the most recoverable coal reserves than any other single country.

- The coal found in the USA accounts for 25% of all economically and technologically recoverable reserves for the entire world.

- Coal is the most widely distributed fossil fuel worldwide and it exists on all seven continents of this planet.

- Coal consumption throughout this world population has steadily increased at a slow rate ever since 1970.

- Coal has been discovered in 37 different States of the USA.

- Most of the anthracite (hard) coal is located in the eastern part of the USA, particularly in Pennslyvania.

- Most of the bituminous (soft) coal is located in Kentucky and West Virginia.

- Most of the coal reserves that are east of the Mississippi River are privately owned by people like Muriel's father.

- Today, the top five coal-producing states of the USA are Kentucky, West Virginia, Pennsylvania, Illinois and Ohio.

- Until the year of 1931, Pennsylvania was the leading coal producing state.

- From 1931-1971, West Virginia was the leading coal producing state.

- Since 1971, Kentucky has been the leading coal producing state.

- The proportion of total production coming from the top five coal producing states has, however, steadily decreased from 80% of all USA produced coal in 1965 to approximately 50% in the 1980's.

- This cutback in production has been caused by a growing production of low-sulfur coal from several western states including, Wyoming, Montana, New Mexico, Colorado and North Dakota. The US total coal production from these western states has risen from 5% in 1965 to 20% in 1981.

- Until the year of 1940, over 90% of all coal produced in the United States was from underground mines. Since that time, surface mining is responsible for 60% of all coal that is produced.

- Transportation expenses continue to be the greatest threat to successful coal profits for the Eastern Kentucky mine owners. Consider the following:

In 2008, suppose that the L&N Railroad Company agrees to transport coal from Hazard to Houston for $18.09 per ton. Further, consider that when said coal reaches Houston Light & Power the average delivered cost is as much as $43.98 per ton to HL&P causing an increase of $25.89 per ton over the original price that was paid to the mine owners, like Miss Muriel Combs.

TABLE I -TRANSPORTATION COSTS FOR SOFT COAL SHIPPED BY THE RAILROAD AND THE YEAR INVOLVED.
(Source: EIA-923 Data)

Year	$/ton	$/ton	Percent
2008	18.09	43.98	41.13
2009	16.96	46.26	36.66
2010	18.26	46.87	38.96
2011	19.97	48.64	41.05
2012	20.30	47.37	42.85
Mean:	18.72	46.62	40.15
Item:	(1)	(2)	(3)

ITEM (1) = Average transportation cost.
ITEM (2) = Average delivered cost.
ITEM (3) = Transportation cost of delivered cost in percent.

Theorem One: (1) ÷ (2) = (3) [Valid]
Theorem Two: (1) = (2) x (3) [Valid]

One way of evaluating data of the aforementioned type (as in Table I) is to determine the percent difference (PD) between different related observations. In this case, PD = the data difference divided by their mean.

PD of 2008 = 43.98- 18.09 divided by the
following: (43.98 + 18.09) ÷ 2 or

PD = 43.98- 18.09 ÷ (43.98 + 18.09)/2 or

25.89/31.04 = 83.41 percent difference and the data
is highly significant on a statistical basis.

That huge PD result tells you why the mine owners hate the L&N Railroad who was slowly choking off their livelihood, bit by bit or should I say ton by ton? There is another disturbing fact about the coal business vs. the Railroad.

For the year of 2008, let $18.09 per ton be the cost of moving coal that Miss Murial had to pay the L&N Railroad. Also let $43.98 be the delivery cost that Miss Murial also had to bear to transport to a given customer, like Houston Light and Power Company.

Therefore, one can assume that the following computations are relevant:

($43.98 - $18.09) = ($25.89) and
($25.89 − $18.09) = ($7.80 per ton)

Surprisingly, that sum of $7.80 per ton is not accounted for in Muriel's business records. Where did that sum of money go and in whose bank accounts did it end up in? My mind will always be very curious as to where that pile of money went and who might still be spending some of it? It smells of being some form of payback by party or parties that are, as yet, still unknown. I asked Murial to explain this specific entry but she just smiled and took me to bed. As we became more and more mature, sex seems to be her answer for almost everything

The aforementioned analyses by the EIA is a lot of technical data that is full of fuzzy logic so, I won't bore my readers anymore regarding something that is this complicated. However, I will argue that if, it not understandable by me (a former college professor), then too much talk about that subject will kill my novel's flow and this much I do understand. As the sun sets in the blue horizon, so shall we say goodbye to Form EIA-923. I promise to not use it again during the rest of this particular story. And, I do so because it is best described as more fuzzy logic from our own US Government.

If I had one nice thing to say about Form EIA-923, I would readily admit that it opens the door to claims that the mining business is being slowly threatened by the Railroad business. Unfair and unrealistic shipping costs will, one day make the coal business subservient to the Railroad business and that must never be allowed to occur or exist. As my friend Jack Fitz (a coal mine owner) once said on TV, "Everytime that I make a shipment of several cars of coal, the distribution costs are always higher. When will these transportation costs by the railroad ever stabilize?"

Jack, I am afraid that this will never happen because this struggle is a three-pronged market place where each prong is after the other prong's profits. These are the primary players in this great struggle for both control and ownership:

The Coal Mine Owners Against The L&N
Railroad Against The End User.
Or
The End User Against The L&N Railroad
Against The Coal Miner Owners.

Here, large sums of money are invested So, you can well imagine the trickery that is involved by these three players. And, the number of combinations are (3 x 2 x 1) or 6 different combinations. It's enough to drive Muriel crazy were I not there to help her through this mess. And, since I am now managing her properties on a full-time basis, part of my salary includes magnificent sex and, as far as I am concerned, our sex together is what bonds us together. If any man tries to come between the two of us, I would be strongly tempted to kill that dirty bastard. This is to say that I was and, will always be a very jealous person.

Chapter Four

TWIST

As you might easily imagine, I became a very skillful manager of Muriel's mining properties. I treated those holdings as if they were my very own and I maintained every possible effort to ensure that they would cover her expenses until after she died and passed on to that great divide which separates mankind from both body and spirit. She could always rely on me to make the correct decision that would best serve her interests, not mine or anyone else's.

I loved her primarily for the great sex which we had together. She was dynamic in bed or on a blanket outdoors and, I would never pursue any improvement from the other females that populated the Perry County District. Simply stated, she was mine and I was hers. And, may no one ever come between us, be it our friend or foe and man or woman.

As a function of time, it became more obvious that she was using me for my business acumen, my keen insight and my raw intelligence.

Her coal mines were more profitable than ever before. I was apparently making her happy in bed but, she seemed to want more than I was able to provide. Was she faking an orgasm with me or was she not? Then, what was it that my Muriel really wanted from me, her closest admirer? During one night together, we had a very meaningful discussion about our relationship. These were the points that we both discussed:

MC: Charles, I hate to tell you this but, I do feel somewhat smothered by you and this town of Hazard and all of the citizens whom we call our closest acquaintances. I feel the need to make a large change in the life that we now live.

CH: You have plenty of money so, we could travel the world over if you wish.

MC: No, traveling the world over isn't the answer that I seek.

CH: We could get married, if that's what you want.

MC: No, marriage is not the answer either.

CH: We could build a nice mansion on top of the highest hill, if that's what you want.

MC: No, I need no large mansions that seem to touch the sky.

CH: You could run for some political office and have additional friends if you like.

MC: No, I need no other friends since I already have more so-called friends than I can handle.

CH: We could go on separate cruises to the tropics if that's what you prefer.

MC: No, Troublesome Creek is enough water for me. If I went on a cruise, I would probably get sea sick.

CH: You and I have been very close together for so many years. Do you feel that we need some time apart from each other?

MC: Yes, I believe that a trial separation might prove to be helpful for both of us.

CH: My God, I could never make such a statement about you or to you. We have been together since the first grade and I am happy with our arrangement. And, for many long years, you were also happy. Pray tell, what happened to the two of us?

MC: I don't really know how to answer that question but, I do know this much, I desperately need a change.

CH: Is there another man that is here involved?

MC: Yes, I did have a small fling with Marshall Brown which didn't amount to much but it did light my fire and served to increase my desire for more sex with other men. Darling, will you please release me?

CH: Only if, I must do so.

MC: At this time in my life, I feel the need to go and live somewhere else and start all over with other men. You can still manage my Black Gold holdings but, if I move to Florida, as all of the rich people from Hazard are inclined to do, you must send me part of my earnings each month and, the rest of my income you can keep for yourself. You have been a very close friend since we first met in the first grade and I have no desire to drop you as my trustworthy business partner.

CH: If you choose to follow the pattern that was set by the Hagan's, the Gorman's and the Dixon's, I will make the arrangements that will be necessary to cover all of your expenses in Florida. I will open up a new account called 'Florida' and your father's coal mines can pay for your extended stay in Fort Meyers, Florida or wherever you choose to reside.

MC: Thank you, Charles for being so kind to me. You have been the best friend that a young girl could ever have and that covers all the years since 1938.

CH: Please reconsider and stay here with me. I will do anything to keep you by my side forever until death do us part.

MC: You have done enough, my dear. And, perhaps, you have spoiled me to the point that I want to spread my own wings and fly away to be completely-free of any and all such hindrances.

CH: Am I nothing more than a loving hindrance to you my dear Muriel?

MC: In a certain way Charles, you have hindered my growth and development as a woman.

CH: How so, my dear?

MC: You have controlled my life to the point that I now feel over-controlled. And, I feel the need to be free. Please set me free, my love, all right?

CH: I hope that you are not asking for complete freedom because if, you leave me on that basis, I might as well shoot myself with my Luger pistol and put an end to everything that I hold as being so precious; namely, you and only you.

MC: I understand your love for me but, I feel like I am living in a glass house where, at any moment, my walls will quickly shatter.

CH: I am here to make certain that your house will always stand strong and ever remain erect.

MC: I understand that and I thank you for taking care of my needs since 1938 when we first met. You have done well and, maybe, too well. Perhaps, your over-protection is what I am trying to escape from. At this point in my life, I don't know the cause of my frustration but, believe me, I do know that we must stop seeing so much of each other.

CH: You could have a valid point, my dear Muriel because so many separated couples argue that absence makes the heart grow fonder.

MC: That is exactly why I am asking for a break in our unbridled affair. It is almost too much for me to bear and I do seek another place to rest and recoup from any of my over-strained anxieties.

CH: Muriel, my dear. I never saw this one coming but, whatever you want is fine with me. I will love you forever even if it is nothing more than a long distance relationship that rapidly weakens with time.

MC: Really, Charles! You will let me be free from your grasp and control? I expected an argument over this but, my bags are packed and I will fly to Florida on tomorrow morning. Thank you so much for being so kind to me.

Next day, I drove her to the Perry County Airport and, afterwards, I cried for three straight days, non-stop. Margo Evans had flown her to the Lexington Bluegrass Airport and our close connection was thereby ended. From now on, I would be nothing but her coal mines administrator. And, that was next to nothing, by comparison. I wanted Muriel's love, not her money.

Chapter Five

LOSS

Without Muriel Combs at or near my side, my minutes seemed like hours and my days were more like months or years. Of course, I still have my office work for the Combs Mining Company to do but, that is not enough to completely subdue the pain of this solitude and my bitter aloneness.

I missed her so much that I thought I might kill myself so that the problem of her being so far away from me would no longer be a reality. I just couldn't function properly with the pain of her being no longer close to me. But, then I realized that, if I did commit suicide, there would be no chance at all to win her back so, I decided that some occasional contact is better than no interaction at all. Because, what is now unlikely might someday become a reality, as the poets might claim.

> *My days are too bold,*
> *My nights are too cold.*
> *I have no Muriel,*
> *To make things seem so swell.*

> - Charles Hays 2015

I asked myself what my options were but, I didn't appreciate the answers that my brain returned to me.

- I could go to Florida and have it out with her but, she would argue that she has been there in Fort Meyers for only three weeks.

- I could go to Florida and plead for her return but, she would say, grow up Charles, because I have been here in Fort Meyers for only three weeks.

- I could put a stop on her monthly allowance of spending money but, she would just hire a new coal mine manager and, hurriedly so.

- I could write her a letter to tell her how lost I was without her but, she would just laugh and say, grow up Charley, things can never be as they once were. We all live with changing events that surround us so, why can't you adapt?

- I could advertise in the Fort Meyer's newspaper concerning my loss but, she would be overly embarrassed by such a public approach.

- I could send her some candies and flowers but, she would just say don't bother. The flowers will wilt and I don't need the calories. And, she might say, don't waste my money with such foolishness.

- I could hire a Mexican assassin to kill off all of her lovers. But, that might hurt a person of interest whom I know because the

Fort Meyers area is so full of citizens who have retired there to live in the Sun Belt area. Each of them did, at one time or the other, live in or around the City of Hazard KY. And, Muriel is a lovely girl that attracts men as a magnet is attracted to the North Pole.

- I could fake a fire in one of her mines and ask for her return to Hazard to address the related law suits but, I couldn't make myself tell such a lie, not to her, not ever. If I did lie to her, it would be the first lie that I ever told her and I have no desire to start the prevarication cycle. And, besides, she would just remind me that any 'fire in the hole' was my responsibility, not hers.

- I could hire a Private Detective to follow her around and keep me posted on the sordid details of whom she was having sex with but, I loved her too much to drag her image into the gossip mills of Fort Meyers or beyond.

- I could ask my Aunt Mina who lives in Fort Meyers to intervene on my behalf but, I hesitated to do that because her golden years should not be disturbed by my trivial problems with me trying to keep a long-distance courtship alive and functional.

- I could also ask my Aunt Canzalia who lives in Tampa to have a look-see on my behalf but I didn't want to bother her with any of my foolish notions that Muriel was, in fact, cheating on me.

- I could hire Don Harrods (an old college friend) that lives in Pensacola to take a look-see for me and to privately report back to me about any significant discoveries. But, the last that I heard, Don was having some serious health problems of his own to deal with. So, I chose to leave him alone and let things remain as they are, for the present.

- I could hire an airplane to fly a banner over her house which says, "I love you, Muriel." But, I know that she wouldn't approve and that she would probably call me a silly hillbilly. Plus, she would surely add, that the airplane expense comes out of your wallet, not my purse.

- I could hire some low-life individual to plant some recording devices inside of her home so that I would remain better informed about her amorous habits. But, I backed off of that when I asked myself what would I do if my own privacy was mistreated in this manner? When my inner being told me that I would probably kill the rascal who bugged my dwelling, I relented and did away with the so-called placement of listening devices in her home. That's taking an unfair advantage with my ex-lover in Florida and I won't stand for it, even if I am the guilty party.

- I could have plastic surgery done to alter my appearance enough that she wouldn't recognize me when I was in Florida and checking up on her night time activities. But, I scrubbed that idea when I remembered that she liked my old appearance and I had the fear that she might not like my new appearance. So, in this regard, I did absolutely nothing beyond praying to get my lover back and away from all those other men. She is mine, damn it, and I am a very jealous person who aims to get revenge, if and when I can.

- I could hire Muriel's personal maid as my informant who might, for cold cash, relay key information regarding each man that Muriel took to bed. But, that proved to be inadvisable because her maid was a Cuban refugee who was in dire fear of being exiled back to Castro's Cuba. With the threat of deportation hovering over her head, I doubt very much that the maid would do anything which might cause her to lose her job of working for her employer, Miss Muriel.

- I could hire a retired boxing champion or an ex-football player to stalk her male visitors for the purpose of breaking some fingers and bones. But that wouldn't work if her lovers were the live-in type. Clearly, I needed more detailed information about Muriel's typical lovers before I could finalize my plan of attack for winning her back or getting some sweet revenge against my competition.

- I could try to fan the flames of our former romance a little more by going down to Florida and romancing the stone. This thought was very appealing but, it was also cost-intensive since there would then be no one to run her coal mines for her. Sadly, if I am not around to kick some ass and make the miners earn their pay, there would be no coal mine to manage or worry about. I was married to her coal mine and, I didn't yet realize that.

- I could ask her to marry me as I had done so many times in the past. But her answer was always the same. She said, I want a few years of fun before I settle down and get married to anyone. In brief, she liked her whiskey too much and, I feared that she had become nothing more than a whiskey whore or a bar addict.

- I could ask Muriel to seek some help at an alcohol treatment center. But, I am almost certain that she would remain in complete denial by claiming, "There is no monkey on my back."

- I could marry some fair maiden who lives in Hazard, Kentucky and forget all about my lovely employer who lives in far off Fort Meyers, Florida. But, that would settle only one problem. I could have local sex instead of masturbation but, in the long range, that would lead to continued disappointment since I loved only my sweet Muriel Combs.

To boil the cabbage down, I was a trapped bachelor who had no way to turn except to the South and I couldn't do that because her coal mines would suffer if I left the area. I felt as if I was damned if I stayed and damned if I went. And, straddling the fence while I decided to do something wouldn't help the situation one damned bit.

Chapter Six

MISERY

The saga of Muriel being down there in Florida and me being up here in Hazard is slowly pulling me apart, dragging me down and killing me softly.

- I've seen rich men beg and now I am begging her to return to me.

- I've watched good men die and now I am dying for her embrace.

- I've seen tough men cry and now, I'm the one that is crying my eyes out over her.

- I've seen losers win but not for me because I have lost the only woman that I ever loved.

- I've seen sad people grin but my sadness has no mirth to display.

- I've heard honest men tell lies but I still prefer to tell the truth.

- I've seen the good side of bad and the bad side of good.

- I've beaten my foes and some of them have beaten me.

- I've had my losses and my gains.

- I've loved the worst dames at least a couple of times. Until I broke their heart or they broke mine.

- I've drunk from the golden cup and I've licked the silver spoon.

- If I didn't have my bad luck, I would have had no luck at all.

- I've stroked the worst curls of several girls.

- I've seen the downside of good people and the upside of better people.

- I've been to some good places but, sadly, I've been to a number of bad places.

- I've hurt some girls before they have hurt me.

- I've helped more girls than I have hurt.

- I've never struck a woman even though some women have seriously tempted me to do so.

- I've loved my mother and I have cared for her in her old age. At the end of the day, she lived in a fine nursing home.

- I've also loved my father and I gave him a fine funeral and burial. I buried him where he needed to be, on flat ground so that I could travel to the Cemetery and visit with him.

- I've learned the thickness and the diameter of every coin, including even the lowly penny.

- I've stroked the meanest of dames at least a couple of times.

- I've tamed the wildest of beasts and some of them were redheads.

- I've heard that blondes have more fun but none of my women ever complained.

- I've been to war and back but, the best place to be is here, not there.

- I've known how to start things but I need help on how to end things.

- I see things as they are, not what I would prefer them to be.

- I've lived through the greatest of recessions (1929-1939) and I am still depressed.

- I've met my match and Muriel has out-matched me.

- I could use a sweet taste of honey moonshine but, it's too hot for the bees.

- I've a liking for Coke and she prefers Pepsi so we could be forever ill-fated or star-crossed.

- I've plenty of canned beans but, she prefers peas and that could be one of our problems.

- I've survived the worst of storms and hurricanes but I still have trouble with the worst of the best women.

- I've a preference for blue skies and white clouds but, sometimes even Mother Nature lets me down or disappoints me.

- I've a strong desire for a great fortune but, I am currently stuck with a larger poverty.

- I've an interest in acquiring more gold but, for me, it will have to be either Black Gold or Fool's Gold (Pyrite).

- I've taken the firm position that only Muriel will suffice for me so, all other women must be properly advised, please stay away from me. It is Muriel that I want and no other woman will be enough.

- I've witnessed the good, the bad and the ugly but, which of them best describes Muriel? At the drop of a hat, she can be pretend to be either one of the three.

- I've heard the wind whistling 'come back to me' but Muriel never pays any attention to the wind.

- I've talked to her on the telephone but, most of what I do is to listen and take orders.

- I've watched Muriel's image in the reflection pond but, then, the frog jumps and her image is gone again.

- I've seen the best and the worst but none can be better than her.

- I've traveled a long journey and I need her to console me.

- I've played a lot of different roles but I have wanted only one, to be Muriel's lover.

- I've loved many women and I have lost but one.

- I've tasted the best wines and none can compare to the taste of her beautiful lips.

- I've met women from six continents and none of them please me as much as Muriel does.

- I've drowned myself in misery by wanting you and needing you.

- I've almost lost my cheerfulness over losing you to the Sun Belt.

- I've devoted my life to you and what you desire but I want more, I want you.

- I've spent years developing a fondness between the two of us and now, I fear that we are drifting apart.

- I've tried to capitalize on every opportunity to make you my wife but, you only want me to manage your properties. What's in this arrangement that benefits me other than my salary?

- I've participated in every event that you have asked of me but, this long-distance affair is wearing me down.

- I've financed almost every material possession that you have requested. When will you accept me as your ever loving sponsor?

- I've gained your trust. When may I have your complete devotion?

- I've known about your current boyfriends for some time. When will it be like the old days of just you and me?

- I've learned about life and most of it is painful. The things that we do to each other are sometimes too awful to discuss.

- I've lost contact with the golden rule. If I treat you nice, why don't you treat me likewise?

- I've learned that other couples give and take. Why is it that you only take and rarely give?

- I've felt the downside and I've loved the upside. Can't we somehow linger in between?

Chapter Seven

TRIP

Math professors would claim that both Muriel and I are living with an inverse relationship which is strongly affected by distance. Their expression would state that

$$LOVE = 1/DISTANCE.$$

As we grow farther apart, our mutual attraction dwindles. However, as we get close or closer to each other, the relationship heats up in a manifold manner.

After reading some of those familiar equations, I became convinced that, if I wanted to save what little we had left between us, I needed to visit the Sun Belt area of Florida. So, I gathered my bare essentials together in an old Samsonite piece of luggage as I planned a surprise trip to the Fort Meyers area.

I drove to Lexington, KY and left my car at the Bluegrass Airport because I didn't want to alert Margo Evans that I was going to visit her best friend, Muriel Combs. I wanted my arrival to be a surprise visit, if possible. I suspected Muriel of some 'hanky-panky' so I needed additional proof to back up any of my so-called accusations. And, I felt that the best way to obtain such information was if I was either crafty or cunning.

The trip was long and tiring such that my claustrophobic tendencies were aroused to the maximum level of my embarrassment. I changed planes in Atlanta for which reason, I know not why. It would have been far more reasonable to have used one plane, not two. But, who am I to wonder why. Southwest Airlines is Southwest Airlines and there is nothing that I can do to change that. From Lexington to Atlanta to Fort Meyers, I ignored as much as I could.

Finally, I arrived at the airport of Fort Meyers, FL and the inspection of my baggage became a moveable feast to recall forever and beyond. The security agent (SA) who inspected my luggage had several witticisms to offer; namely,

SA: What's this bottle of pills for?

CH: That's my VIAGPURE. It is supposed to help me with my ability to have sex.

SA: Have you looked at the contents?

CH: No, not lately, why?

SA: It contains a lot of things that could be harmful to your health, like Goat Weed, Acai Berry Extract, Psyillum Husk, Dandelion Root, Allalfa Leaf, Garcinia Cambogia Fruit, Green Coffee Bean Extract, Raspberry Ketone African and Mango Extract.

CH: In my case, I feel like the reward of having good sex is more than worth the risk of taking that pill.

SA: What's this bottle of pills for?

CH: That's my ROCKHARD pills. They are supposed to help me with an increased size of my penis, an improved erection, better stamina and more staying power.

SA: Have you looked at these contents?

CH: No, not lately, why?

SA: It contains some mighty special stuff that could be harmful to your health, like sarsaparilla powder, pumpkin seed powder, muria puama powder, oat straw powder, nettle powder, cayenne pepper powder, astragalus powder, catauba bark powder, licorice, tribulus terrestris powder, orchic, oyster extract, boron, gelatin, calcium carbonate and magnesium stearate. For example, that sarsaparilla stuff used to be used for liver disease and syphilis, did you not know that?

CH: No I did not but, I repeat myself. The reward of good sex is worth the risk.

SA: What's this bottle of pills for?

CH: That's my natural testosterone booster and it's supposed to increase my sex drive, enhance my muscle mass and boost my free testosterone.

SA: Have you considered the contents?

CH: No, not lately, why?

SA: It's contains some weird stuff such as zinc chelate, vitamin B 6, vitamin B 12, testone fenugreek extract, fernuside, L citrulllline malate, gelatin and magnesium stearate. In other words, it is alphabet soup with no saltines.

CH: I say again, the reward of good sex is worth the risk that I take.

SA: What is this bottle of pills for?

CH: That's my male potency tonic and it is called XTREME TESTRONE. And, before you ask, it contains some pretty unusual contents; namely,

- Horny Goat Weed Leaf,
- Tongkat Aki root extract,
- Saw Palmetto root extract,
- Orchic substance,
- Wild yam root extract,
- Sarsaparilla root extract,
- Nettle root extract,
- Boron Amino Acid Chelate, Calcium
- Calcium Carbonate,
- Microcrystalline Cellouse,
- Stearic Acid and
- Magnesium Stearate.

SA: Which brings us to this bottle, called EXTREME 2000. Pray tell, what is it used for?

CH: That's my dietary supplement which is supposed to help me with my workouts at the local YMCA fitness center.

SA: Have you considered the contents of this bottle? It is a fantastic collection of alphabet soup. Can you tell me what these terms mean? If you can't, I may have to confiscate them in order to protect Fort Myers from any and all suspect substances. We are trying our best to keep Fort Meyers free of all suspicious drugs and any undefined chemicals.

- L-Arginine Alpha Ketoglutarate,
- L-Arginine Ketoisocaproate,
- L-Ornithine Alpha Ketoglutarate,
- L-Glutomine Alpha Ketoglutarate
- Gelatin,
- Di-Calcium Phosphate,
Magnesium Stearate and
Silicon Dioxide.

SA: And, now we come to this last bottle of pills called PHGH. What in the hell is this used for?

CH: PHGH is needed for the capillaries of my penis. This pill is supposed to enlarge the capillaries so that more blood flow can exist inside my middle leg. Thereby, I can have improved sex with a larger penis which well be harder for a longer time.

SA: I studied chemistry in high school but, I never heard of these chemicals before. Mister Hays, do you feel safe when you put all of these constituents into your stomach?

CH: When I take them, I do feel a drop in my blood pressure but, until now, I have always attributed that problem to anxiety while I am watching my lady friend undress. You know what, you are causing me some real concern over these pills that I have been buying from the Internet.

SA: I should think so. Just take a look at what your PHGH contains. It's loaded with unknown chemicals and suspicious sounding compounds like the following:

- L-Arginine,
- TribulusTerrestris Extract,
- Tonkat Ali Extract,
- L-Carnitine,
- DHEA,
- Catuba Bark Extract,
- Horny Goat Weed,
- Ginkgo Leaf,
- Maca Root Extract,
- Muira Puama Herb and
- Black Pepper Extract.

SA: Man, it's a wonder that you aren't pickled from the inside to the outside!

Charles Hays

CH: Angrily I said, can I go now?

SA: No Sir. I am not letting this stuff enter our fair city. You might leave it laying around and we citizens here in Fort Meyers might have us one of them epidemics, like Ebola. Where did you fly in from?

CH: I told him that I had flown in from Hazard Kentucky and that I was a coal mine operator.

SA: That does it for me. I lost a third cousin in one of them coal mine disasters and I'm still pissed off, even today.

CH: I am just here to see my girlfriend and I didn't have anything to do with harming your third cousin. I am sorry for your loss. Now, can I go?

SA: Nope, this stuff and that old suitcase will be burned in our brand new incinerator this very evening.

Of course, I was extremely angry. That old suitcase had been in the family since the 1940's. I asked him one final question and it included these words, Is there a GNC store in Fort Meyers? He didn't reply with a single word. Instead, he handed me a business card that read, ELMER'S GNC STORE at 632 Broadway Street in Fort Meyers. At that point, I separated myself from that Security Guard as soon as was possible. His name badge told me that his name was Elmer Gantry and that he was merely re-stocking his store shelves at my expense.

Oh, the games people play now,
Every night and every day now,
Never meaning what they say now,
Never meaning what they mean now.

Chapter Eight

ATTEMPT

Over the years, I have grown to dislike the word 'attempt'. Instead, I much prefer the word 'accomplish'. Before I retired from the Oil & Gas Industry, I was an experimentalist, who was dedicated to making components better through trial and error, theory and practice or by failure and success.

We material scientists were trying to support a plan that would expose any existing fraud and to eliminate all designed dishonesty or careless cheating. In essence, we were trying to build a perfect product for a longer service time at a cheaper cost. I felt that we engineers were always trying to improve things for the better. So, the word 'attempt' seems almost inappropriate for a hard working metallurgical engineer who was dedicated to solid successes, instead of flimsy attempts or foolish failures.

And, at this time, that retired engineer had traveled to the city of Fort Meyers, FL. And, his most fervent desire was to somehow make Muriel change her ways and to recover their loving relationship back to what it was at an earlier time and place. This was a large responsibility but, as I had said to Elmer Gantry, my risk was well worth my reward.

I wanted her love back since, I felt certain that she was sharing her body with other men, instead of me. That was my reason for being in this wicked place which permitted the theft of souvenir suitcases and all of my personal pills. Yes, I was prepared to stay for as long as it took to win her back. I was ready to fight for her embrace,

I was determined to accomplish my goals and there was no room in my mind for a meager attempt, especially since my life had always been given to succeeding, not just attempting. This was my passion, this was my goal and this was my reason for living. Muriel Combs was everything that I wanted. I desired only her and I didn't crave for anyone else, not even Esther Williams.

I called her phone number and I asked her for an appointment. I lied when I said that my agenda had something to do with her coal mine properties. I told her that we needed to make an important decision relative to surface mining or underground mining. Money and the thought of more money would open any door belonging to my beloved Muriel. She pleaded with me to delay my arrival to her house by one day on the pretext of saying that her house needed a thorough cleaning.

And, against my better judgement, I told her that this would be fine with me since I also wanted to visit my Aunt Mina who lived in the area. Mina had written her own biography and she had given her book the interesting name of 'Flame'. The storyline of Flame was about the many love affairs that Mina had experienced as a beautiful young girl in the small town of Jackson, KY. And dear Mina wanted me to review her book.

After my nice visit with Mina, I went to bed in a downtown hotel room where I was excited about the next day's events. I would be seeing Muriel again after a very long interval and I was prepared to discuss everything that I could toward the prospect of winning her love back once again.

Obviously, I did not sleep very well that night. Instead, I tossed and turned and I woke up to write down all of the things that I wanted to talk to her about on the following day. In that manner, my night-time thoughts were properly documented and preserved by the use of those little green POST-IT stickers that are always positioned near my bedside lamp.

The reason that the POST-ITs are near my bed is that most of my better book ideas come to me in the middle of the night. And, I have to take notes at night or I will forget my dreams when the time arrives for my Banana Nut Muffin every single morning of every single day.

Now, we come to the nitty and the gritty of our long-awaited first reunion in Florida. I checked out of the hotel and I drove to the mansion where she was living. It was a six bedroom house with an Olympic-sized swimming pool in her backyard on the Western Drive of Fort Meyers. It was not at all typical of her nice home in Hazard, KY where she was born and reared. In fact, there was not one house in the Hazard area which could begin to compare to what she was living in at the present time.

My meager background, my simple beginnings, my conservative attitude and my pitiful salary could never serve to impress Murial Combs with respect to her current abode and a party-based lifestyle.

To be quite honest, I was strongly tempted to leave her crowded driveway and go back to my simple homeland in Eastern Kentucky without even talking to her. But, I did have an appointment and I had come this far so, I weathered the storm of curiosity and anxiety to calmly await my turn to speak with her. I was really into this mission and I was very deeply involved. Certainly, I was well past the point of a no-excuse return or a well-mannered exit. If I had an honorable mode of retreat, I should have used it because this mansion and her apparent lifestyle was making me a little sick at my stomach. I never wanted to waste any hard-earned money in the same manner that she was doing.

In my mind, I pictured the miner with a jackhammer in his hands working his life away for this big spender and that savvy socialite who went by the name of Muriel Combs. She was the love of my life but, she was losing ground rapidly. She was my type in the first grade but, now she is no longer the same person. This mansion, these cars, and the associated property reminded me of something right out of the Great Gatsby and I didn't exactly appreciate what I was viewing.

Now, I had more than just one objective of winning back her love and affection. Somehow, I needed to remind her of the pending possibilities that we were facing if we went after more coal by surface mining methods instead of continuing with ancient underground techniques.

I rang the doorbell and a cute little house maid invited me inside of that great mansion. Muriel met me in the Grand Room and she was sprawled onto the luxury of a mink-covered lounging chair. Muriel was smoking with an extended cigarette holder and that was a new addiction for her because she had never smoked in front of me before, not once.

She said hello and pointed toward the couch as if to say, you sit there and adore me old friend. Next, she abruptly added, I can give you no more than ten minutes because I am scheduled for a pedicure after this is over. I was being treated like the railroad trash that I am and, I didn't care for such treatment, not one bit. I hate snobbery and I always have. Then, I began with my spiel:

CH: I want you to return to the mountains with me. I love you, I miss you and I want you at my side, again.

MC: Surely, you jest. I am very comfortable here in Florida with my mansion, my live-in friends and all of my material possessions. Why should I leave all of this for a return to that land of wretched poverty?

CH: Because, I asked you to do this for me and my well-being. We were happy once and we can be happy again.

MC: I am happy here but, at Hazard, I would be bored to death. Here, I can drink wine and dance the night away with one or more of my suitors. There at Hazard, I would be limited to reading a book or watching reruns on an old television set.

CH: I was able to satisfy your needs back then and I can do the same, once again.

MC: Darling, even at your best, you were not a very good sex partner. Your specialty was slam, bam, thank you Ma'am.

CH: Let's change the subject because it is getting a little warm in this room and this topic of discussion badly needs a change. Then, I loosened my collar by a small amount for emphasis.

MC: Are you still set on the concept of surface mining even though it will cost me a large fortune?

CH: To make more money, you have to invest more money.

MC: Then bring that mountain down, honey by any and all means. I need more money and I needed it yesterday.

CH: Here is a check for your earnings during the month of August. This sum is for a total of $100,000 clear profit from all of your mines, will that help?

MC: As she grabbed the check, she said, I expected more but, this will have to do, I guess.

CH: You expected more money and I expected to sleep in your bed for a couple of nights. What have we both become?

MC: You have become my coal mining manager and I have become your employer, nothing more and nothing less.

CH: Outside of my body, I felt like crying but, inside, I felt like slapping her face. In the old days, her tongue was never that sharp or cruel to me.

MC: Then she announced, your ten minutes are over. Will you please leave? I must tend to my toes and you must return to the Hazard coal fields to knock down a few mountains and make me a lot richer. Next time that you decide to deliver a check covering my monthly profits, please remember that I want to make $1,200,000 each and every month since $92,000 per month is not enough. Goodbye old friend. O hope that you have a safe trip back to our original homeland. And, if you are still expecting some sex with me, forget all about that as each of my bedrooms are currently occupied by younger men who don't have to use a penis pump.

CH: I was extremely embarrassed so, I quickly departed from that awful place. And, I promised myself to never grace her front door again. I learned that whatever is currently lost may not be worth finding again.

Chapter Nine

EMPATHY

Fast forward to a few days after my round trip to Florida was completed and you will find me still confused and baffled as to why Muriel should suddenly treat me in a manner that I was totally unaccustomed to. At one time, I was her only lover and now that she has gotten the big head, I am reduced to the level of being just another lowly employee of hers. That business of allowing me only ten minutes time in lieu of an all-important pedicure infuriated me to no end as I finally realized that my bygone days were forever gone.

My love for her was greatly diminished and her love for me was now the folly of other men, each of them being total strangers to me, her lifetime friend and her excellent manager of her Black Gold empire. Instead of making her richer, my immediate intent was to try and make her a whole lot poorer and as soon as possible. I did hold that thought for a few seconds but, I dismissed that idea quite rapidly.

If I weakened with my intent and quickly adopted a negative decline management scheme, what distress would that have on our miners and their families? Because our mining empire was the largest operation of the tri-county area, it would be a colossal disaster that could hurt a lot of innocent people. Therefore, I couldn't bring myself to go in that direction, since our mines served to fill a lot of empty stomachs. It was okay for me to be mad at Muriel but, it was wrong for me to be mad at the families of our dedicated coal miners. They were just innocent bystanders who were caught up in this complicated web of deceit, we mine operators against the L&N railroad, the TVA power plants and the hungry politicians from the western states.

However, and after a considerable amount of concentrated study, I elected to consult some outside medical experts regarding what was wrong with my long distance sweetheart, Miss Muriel Combs of Fort Myers, FL.

- Dr. Leonard Maurer, M.D concluded that Muriel Combs was a victim of a valid nymphomaniac disorder. However, he did say that he was unable to reach a final decision without interviewing the patient on a 1-to-1 basis and in private. He even offered to fly down there to Fort Meyers for a weekend holiday.

- Dr. Maria Landsberry, MD decided that Muriel was being controlled by damaging depressive symptoms. She said that she would have to visit Florida to form a definitive opinion.

- Dr. Ari Narasimhan, MD concluded that there was nothing wrong in having multiple sex partners. And, he even asked for her personal phone number on the basis that he wanted to do some personal interviews via long distance.

- Dr. Naomi Fields, MD recommended that Murial should be under the care of a social psychiatrist. She claimed that she could help my sweetheart because she suffered from the same problem that Muriel did. And, she also added this little tidbit; it sounds as if all your sweetie really needs is a faithful lesbian companion.

- Dr. Sam Fielding suggested that Muriel had a problem with polyandry and he indicated that he was 110% certain of his analysis. That medical problem was his specialty and he was the only one of the five doctors who had an opinion that was this firm. Speaking of which, Sam had an erection throughout our interview. He was really turned on by hearing about Muriel and her antics.

Of these five medical opinions only the one by Dr. Fielding made any real sense to me. Because of his diagnosis, I decided to become better acquainted with concept of polyandry. The best source of information that I could find was taken from Wikipedia – the no-cost encyclopedia and I quote this article almost verbatim.

"Polyandry involves marriage that includes more than two partners and can fall under the broader category of polyamory. More specifically, it is a form of polygamy whereby a woman takes two or more husbands at the same time. In its broadest use, polyandry refers to sexual relations with multiple males within or without marriage."

And, that is exactly what I witnessed when I visited Fort Meyers, multiple men living with Muriel in a house that Black Gold built, in a house that my hard work made possible. I was repulsed by what was going on in Florida. But, what could I do about this bothersome situation?

- I could move to Florida and do a little housecleaning but, that would probably endanger my job as her manager of mines. She no longer loved me as she did once before but, she still admired and needed my brains. That was my job security as far as Muriel was concerned. But, in that regard, I felt as if I was standing in quicksand and harm was on its way.

- I could hire an ex-football player to break a few bones but bones heal and womanizers always return to their base of operations.

- I had saved my money just as a miser would so I was rich enough to buy those men off and make them leave her property. But, they would return to Muriel before I could manage my departure from the Fort Meyers Airport. Good sex is hard to find and that applies for both good guys and bad guys.

- I could arrange for Muriel to have an aggressive lesbian friend of the possessive type. That move might keep Muriel too busy to allow much messing around with her live-in lovers. Unfortunately for me, even lesbians like an occasional screw with a member of the opposite sex. But, that might be like adding more fuel to a hot fire that is already flaming at a maximum burn rate.

- I could send her a harem of beautiful girls to sleep in those six bedrooms with one objective; to keep Muriel's admirers otherwise preoccupied. Their single mission would be to drain those male gonads dry.

- I could have each of her live-in lovers undergo a vasectomy on the pretense that Muriel might avoid cancer if her men were 'fixed'. But what could that possibly do for my insane jealousy? It might serve as revenge but it wouldn't bother me and my wicked thoughts.

- I could have her house torched but, she would just build another home that contained more luxuries and back charge all of those expenses to our mining operations. It would be more cost-effective if I left her lover's house alone and did nothing to damage the property.

- I could try to get her declared as being insane but, if I failed or, if my medical consultants failed me, truth would out and hell would exist.

- I could try to overwhelm her with meaningless paper work but Muriel isn't that dumb. Sooner or later, she would figure out what I was up to and she would say, I am not going to put up with this anymore. You handle this instead of me. That's what you get paid for.

- I could try to make those men to surgically remove their genitals and place them in a glass jar with formaldehyde but that would be like moving a mountain using only a teaspoon so, I gave up that attractive thought.

- I could sabotage her automobiles to try and slow her shopping trips down but she would just buy a limousine with an over-sexed chauffeur.

- I could ask her to become sterilized so that there would be no heirs to foil my plans of taking over the empire but, I abandoned that thought since we were both approaching the point where healthy children could not be spawned by either one of us.

- I could do this or I could do that but, the simplest thing was to do nothing so that's what I did. Muriel had survived a number of years just as she was when I last visited her so, I asked myself, what harm would a few more years do? I decided to hide and watch Fort Myers from afar.

Chapter Ten

REUNION

Our graduating class of 1950 has staged only one class reunion that I know about and that grand celebration occurred during the 1970's, as I recall. It was sponsored by Mayor Gorman and his impressive mansion was the designated meeting site. I remember it very well because I live in Texas and, at the time, I was down with pneumonia when the event was scheduled.

I seldom get sick but that one bout with pneumonia kept me from visiting my former friends and fellow students at our first and only class reunion. I sent my regrets and classmate Don McQuarte was kind enough to send me some photographs that were taken at the scene.

I truly enjoyed seeing how some of my old friends had aged and I got a good look-see of the Mayor's pretentious abode. The most impressive thing about Bill Gorman's residence was that the basement was walled with mirrors from the floor to the ceiling and all around which left most of the guests with an opportunity to judge each other's stature, their over-all profile and general appearance. It wasn't necessary to stare, you could just shift your feet a small amount to get a better view of everyone's complete silhouette by looking at the mirrors instead of looking at directly at them.

The average age of the attendees was just 38-years old but there was ample evidence of premature baldness, skin wrinkles, sagging muscles, bulging tummies and downright obesity. Yes, there was fatness at this early age which surprised me to no end. And, every guest seemed to be overly indulgent for cocktails and hors d'oeuvres to a degree that was apparently excessive. This suggested that no one had eaten any supper prior to that evening's gathering. And, alcohol on an empty stomach.... well, you can imagine the end result of that occurrence.

I next assumed that none of my classmates knew exactly what workouts and exercises really meant. It was cocktails and conversations and strictly a social event as far as I could tell from my independent study of Don's photographic album that he sent to me.

And, from one photograph to another photograph, there was no indication of any hanky-panky going on. All of the girls were accounted for in each picture and none were assumed to be in any upstairs bedroom. And, that surprised me because the females of our 1950 Class had a very healthy attitude regarding intercourse. They weren't nymphos but, most of the girls did enjoy frequent sex more than most other women do.

Some of the girls brought their husbands with them to the reunion and these hubbies were as out-of-place as anyone could be. Therefore, they drifted to a far corner of the basement room where they were aloof and apart from the mainstream conversations which were dominated by Muriel. Otherwise, most of the crowd was congregated in a large separate circle in the center of the room which included the main bunch of ex-Bulldogs from Hazard High School.

But, guess who moved around the most and who was apparently the queen of conversation at this reunion party? It was Muriel Combs, of course. In a stream of e-mails, Don said that she monopolized the entire evening by going from person-to-person and telling each and every one all about her ten husbands since Graduation Day. She had ten husbands in twenty years, Lordy, Lordy! Fortunately for me, Don

M. took excellent notes which he shared with me. That enabled me to write about the following details:

- HUSBAND NUMBER (1): Muriel stated that her first husband was a man that she married out of spite. She and I had experienced a terrible argument about money so she married someone else to just punish me. His name was Orville Wrong and that poor slob had nothing to do with aeroplanes. He was a big strong coal miner with a monumental-sized penis which Muriel liked very much. However, she soon dropped him as a husband, saying that she would rather be tickled to death than stabbed to death.

- HUSBAND NUMBER (2): Murial married a midget who was about one-half her height. And, they divorced because he liked to lick her belly button too much. That was his foreplay but, it was also his downfall as a husband because Muriel grew tired of that in a very short time.

- HUSBAND NUMBER (3): Muriel married a vampire who liked to drink her blood but, she ditched him on the advice of her medical doctor. After a short while, Muriel became grossly deficient in several key blood constituents. For example, her iron content became much too low. It was dump him or die, according to her personal physician.

- HUSBAND NUMBER (4): Muriel married a gigolo who was the only man that could ever satisfy her sexual needs but he became sterile when he could no longer provide any semen. So, she divorced him and started a new search for a younger guy with more fructose in his system. She was told by her doctor that, without fructose, infertility is the end result. And, she was on a high fructose diet.

- HUSBAND NUMBER (5): Muriel married a homosexual who was still in his closet until she outed him. And, that divorce stated that she wanted a real man, not a gay person. The divorce court allowed the separation since the judge took a fancy to Muriel's husband.

- HUSBAND NUMBER (6): Muriel married a hunter of wild game and she divorced him because she couldn't stand the sight of animal heads being attached to each wall of her mansion. And, her husband refused to take them down so that constituted a legal issue of irreconcilable differences. She liked animals but she was frightened by dead ones, especially at night when the mounted ones seemed to be more alive. And, get this, there was four lions mounted in her bedroom. This was more than enough to convince the Divorce Judge who just happened to be an animal lover. This is to also say that the divorce was quickly granted for Muriel.

- HUSBAND NUMBER (7): Muriel married a drug dealer who got her addicted. After, her rehabilitation, she turned him in to the authorities and he is now in a Florida prison serving a long sentence of fifty years. Her divorce from that bastard was uncontested by her husband.

- HUSBAND NUMBER (8): Muriel married a gourmet cook who loved to cook but, unfortunately, he also liked to eat. When he became a heavyweight of 350-lbs, she ditched him as a husband. She told the divorce judge that when she wanted sex, she couldn't find his penis because it was hidden beneath layers upon layers of fatty tissue and large skin tabs or overlaps. She maintained that he also hid his wallet between different folds of fat so that he could keep his money separate from her money. He was a well-paid gourmet cook whose secret recipes were in great demand.

- HUSBAND NUMBER (9): Muriel married a sailor who sailed the ocean blue but one who rarely came home to satisfy her sexual needs and priorities. The divorce judge was a former Army Officer who disliked sailors as much as I did. That divorce was quickly granted for reasons relating to abandonment.

- HUSBAND NUMBER (10): Muriel married a lesbian but all they did was to quarrel about which insertion tool was to be used on which night. Her name was Bambi and she refused to share any of her instruments. And, sometimes, Bambi refused to have sex with Muriel. In brief, she was playing hard to get so, it wasn't long before Muriel left her for another husband who tested high on fructose with a healthy prostate gland and sound seminal vesicles.

She pretty well convinced the reunion crowd that she was either foolish or crazy. However, she was the entertainment for that reunion night. Of this, there can be very little doubt. In a subsequent e-mail, Don McQuarte added that she behaved in that manner because someone had slipped her a pill that made her hyperactive and very silly.

Chapter Eleven

EPILOGUE

Fast forward to the present time so that this old storyteller can tell you what happened to Muriel Combs as she grew older. She had an estate which was worth several million dollars but when she died, she was penniless. I was still her estate manager so I buried her at my own expense since I didn't want my former lover to be buried in a pauper's grave or to have her ashes spread to who knows where, when or why.

Muriel became a philanthropist toward the end of her life. She gave away a lot of money to struggling artists and writers who were desperate for her kind assistance and sponsorship.

- If you wanted to publish a book but couldn't because the expense was beyond your means, just contact Muriel and, within two weeks, a cashier's check to cover that amount would arrive in your mailbox.

- If you wanted to get into politics but, couldn't afford the campaign expenses, Muriel would finance all your needs with no strings attached. And, she didn't take issue with either political party, be it Democrat, Republican or otherwise. However, she had no use for the Communist Party.

- If your child was ill and needed a life-saving surgery at the Mayo Clinic, just contact Muriel and every penny of that expense would be paid for by her and her alone.

- If you needed a nursing home and your children wouldn't help you, ask Muriel and she would find you a nice place to live up to a maximum cost of ten thousand dollars per month.

- If you could no longer manage a car and you required mobility, talk to Muriel and she would buy you a brand new KIA or FIAT.

- If your shoes had holes in their soles, Muriel would buy you some new shoes or have the old ones repaired, whichever you preferred.

- If you could no longer afford your food, Muriel would purchase frozen dinners until you passed away.

- If you needed female companionship, Muriel would make certain that a professional volunteer would visit your residence for eight hours each day so that you would never be completely alone again.

- If you had two children, a son that can't and a daughter that won't, then Muriel would pay for someone to serve as your daytime housekeeper and live-in companion.

- If this book chronicles her accidental experiences with some of the most influential people and important events that occurred in America during the 1950's through the 1970's, then it is safe to state that she walked through life blindly but, she paused long enough to help every needy person that she met.

- What greater goal in life is there other than to help someone who needs your assistance?

- Her gifts were both small and large and the people that received her gifts never knew her real identity.

- She counseled with Citizens, Mayors, Governors and Presidents as if they were her brothers and sisters who needed her help and legal guidance.

- She served as an ambassador of good will to nations that sought her keen insight and good nature.

- She was the first to recognize the hidden dangers of dealing with nuclear treaties which involved the wayward Nation of Iran.

- Muriel's kind heart and never failing love for me taught me more than any University could ever teach me. I was her employee but she was my role model, particularly during the last few months of her life.

- Muriel taught me what my destiny was; to have and to hold, to love and respect, and, moreover, to let small worries remain small. She said, if you can't remember who harmed you yesterday, then forgive everyone today.

- Muriel had several old sayings for me to live my life by and one of them was the following: Don't believe all that you hear but, you must believe what you say.

- Another one was: Some critics are using the only talent that they have and that's why they deserve our pity.

- Another one was: If we reap what we sow, pray for a drought.

- Another one was: Insisting is not a substitute for persisting.

- Another one was: Minorities that only react will seldom act.

- Another one was: One lie begets other lies.

- Another one was: If something can be counted, it counts.

- Another one was: Mean people have more fear.

- Another one was: Trouble tells us what we are.

- Another one was: You don't have to be close to be close.

- Another one was: Deeds say much more than words can promise.

- Another one was: The one unique thing about life is death.

- Another one was: The borrower becomes a slave to the lender.

- Another one was: Lead by giving a good example.

- Another one was: Laugh at that which deserves laughter.

- Another one was: Some people work to live while others live to work.

- Another one was: A good education is expensive but, it does pay off.

- Another one was: Words that must be eaten are hard to digest.

- Another one was: Never laugh at your own jokes.

- Another one was: Nothing is ever completely one-way.

- Another one was: If you desire friends, try being one first.

- Another one was: Know when to be brave and when to be smart.

- Another one was: The boldest puppy of the litter gets the most attention.

- Another one was: Leaders act and followers react.

- Another one was: Be as snug as a bug in a rug if you can.

- Another one was: Approval fuels self-esteem.

- Another one was: Any age is the right age to improve your life.

- Another one was: Too many people believe that more is better.

- Another one was: No debt is due at just the right time.

- Another one was: If you can't do anything else, practice law.

- Another one was: Thoughtful and thoughtless are two widely different approaches.

- Another one was: Not as you were or as you are but, as you ought to be.

- Another one was: Railroaders have this saying, steam will rise only if the shovel is full of coal.

- Another one was: No sooner said than done but, sooner done than argued.

- Another one was: For an idea whose time has come, its hour will soon pass.

- Another one was: Never say 'that is why' without explaining 'why that is'.

- Another one was: She was sweet as honey but, sometimes, as sour as vinegar.

- Another one was: Wisdom returns when concentration resumes.

- Another one was: No one plans to fail. They just fail to plan.

- Another one was: Power naps are needed if a full day is required.

- Another one was: Measure once and cut twice. Measure twice and cut once.

- Another one was: Brevity is the soul of wit.

- Another one was: Never beat a dead horse.

- Another one was: Above all, try to be above most.

- Another one was: Disagree without being rude.

- Another one was: The shorter live longer than the longer.

- Another one was: Money can't buy love but, money can buy a politician.

- Another one was: The larger the lake, the greater the pollution.

- Another one was: The mortician's creed is 'better thee than me'.

- Another one was: Tie a knot to keep a thought.

- Another one was: Never try to brush someone's hair while you are angry.

- Another one was: If you can afford to buy the meat, don't hunt.

- Another one was: One good day redeems many bad days.

- Another one was: Women cannot keep secrets.

- Another one was: A women's real education begins with marriage.

- Another one was: To discover a Robin's nest that contains eggs is a sign of good luck.

- Another one was: To be happy you must first want happiness.

- Another one was: Night air is considered to be evil air.

- Another one was: If you must write, write as much as you can.

- Another one was: No one asks to be born.

- Another one was: When you take a picture of someone, you trap their soul.

- Another one was: Democracy requires a lot but delivers more.

- Another one was: It wasn't raining when Noah started building his arc.

- Another one was: A college class is defined as ignorance in motion.

- Another one was: We can split the atom but we can't unite the people.

- Another one was: Keep your nose close to the grinding wheel.

- Another one was: Anything finished is better than something which is unfinished.

- Another one was: What is expensive we revere too much.

- Another one was: If you are looking for guidance, don't look elsewhere.

- Another one was: Beauty and brains rarely co-exist in one woman.

- Another one was: First you grow up and, second, you grow out.

- Another one was: It is wise to always become better, not worse.

- Another one was: Marry the woman that you love and love only your wife.

Printed in the United States
By Bookmasters